Tl

Young Knight

BOOK BELONGS TO

....

The Day the Hippo Landed

Young Knight

URSULA DANIELS

The Day the Hippo Landed

illustrated by
Robin Kramer

HODDER AND STOUGHTON

British Library Cataloguing in Publication Data

Daniels, Ursula
  The day the hippo landed.
  I. Title   II. Kramer, Robin
823.914 [J]

ISBN 0-340-53341-2

First published 1988 by Hodder and Stoughton Children's Books
Young Knight edition first published 1991

Published by Hodder and Stoughton Children's Books,
a division of Hodder and Stoughton Ltd,
Mill Road, Dunton Green, Sevenoaks, Kent TN13 2YA
Editorial office: 47 Bedford Square, London WC1B 3DP

Printed in Great Britain by Cambus Litho, East Kilbride

One Saturday afternoon, Sam saw a small speck in the sky. It grew bigger and bigger. At first it looked like a fly. Then a bird. Then a dragon.

Finally he saw that it was really a helicopter. And something very strange was dangling below it.

'Whatever is it?' Dad asked, peering up at the sky.

'It's a large net with something inside it,' said Mum.

Sam stared hard. 'I think it's a hippopotamus,' he said.

Mum and Dad laughed. 'It can't be,' they exclaimed together. But — it *was* a hippo! And the hippo was far too heavy for the helicopter.

The helicopter came lower and lower.

'I hope it doesn't land on the clean hankies,' said Mum anxiously.

'Or in the new pond,' said Dad.

The helicopter came even lower. When it was right over Sam's house, the hippo landed on the roof. And sat there.

The helicopter hovered above. Then with
a *CRACK* and a *CLATTER* and a *CRASH*,
the hippo went through the roof . . .
and through the rafters . . .
and through the loft . . .
and through the ceiling . . .
and landed on Sam's bed.

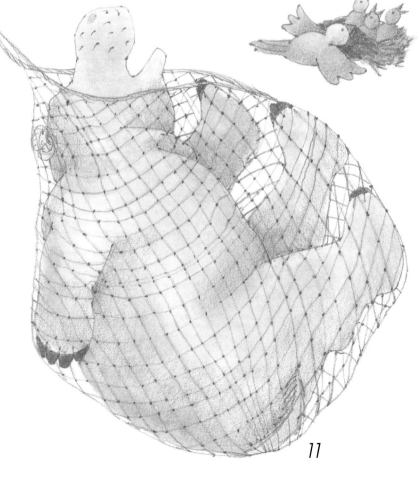

The man in the helicopter untied the ropes that had been holding the net. 'I'll be back,' he yelled and the helicopter flew away.

'At least it missed the hankies,' said Dad.

'And the pond,' said Mum.

'But it's in MY bedroom,' Sam complained loudly. 'So where will I sleep tonight?'

'The helicopter man promised to come back,' said Dad calmly.

They stood and waited
and watched the sky. All the
neighbours came out to stare.
    The hippo sat on Sam's bed
with big, sad eyes.

'He must be feeling lost,' said Mum.

'Perhaps he needs some dinner,' Sam suggested and ran to the kitchen. He found some old toasted crumpets and an ice-cream cornet and some bangers and mash.

Dad climbed up a ladder. He threw the crumpets into Sam's bedroom. The hippo ignored them.

'He doesn't like old toasted crumpets,' said Sam.

So Dad threw the ice-cream cornet to the hippo. The hippo wouldn't touch it.

'He doesn't like ice-cream cornets,' said Sam.

Dad pushed the plate of bangers and mash through the window. The hippo just stared mournfully.

'He doesn't like bangers and mash,' said Sam. 'I wonder what hippos *do* like to eat?'

'Maybe he's not hungry,' said Mum. 'He's got a very fat, full tummy. The important thing is — HOW are we going to get him down?'

Nobody knew.

'Well, he's too fat to come down the stairs . . .'

'And he can't get through the window . . .'

'We'll just have to take down the outside wall!' said Mr Mack from next door.

'My bedroom wall?' asked Sam in a small voice, but no one took any notice.

They fetched ladders and chisels. Soon a whole row of people were chipping away at Sam's bedroom wall.

CHIP. . . CHIP . . . CHIP . . .

'Keep that cement dust off the hankies,' Mum shouted.

'Watch the bits of brick don't go into the pond,' Dad added.

CHIP . . . CHIP . . . CHIP . . .

'We'll have no house left,' said Sam.

CHIP . . . CHIP . . . CHIP . . .

The hippo watched with big, wide eyes.

Bricks began to drop one by one. Soon Sam's bedroom wall lay in a heap in the garden.

I hope it doesn't rain tonight, he thought. With no roof and no wall . . .

What next? Everyone looked at Mr Mack.

'Somehow we have to get him down,' said Mr Mack slowly. 'But how?'

'It's too high to jump,' Mum stated firmly.

'That's it!' said Dad. 'We need something to break his fall.'

'MATTRESSES,' yelled Mr Mack.

Everyone rushed to their houses. Nearly everyone came back dragging a mattress. Mattresses for double beds and for single beds . . . thin, thick, flowery, plain. A garden full of mattresses.

'Come on down,' said Mr Mack.

Everyone joined in. 'Come on down.'

The hippo didn't budge. No one knew what to do next.

Suddenly they heard a small sound that grew louder and louder. It was a helicopter.

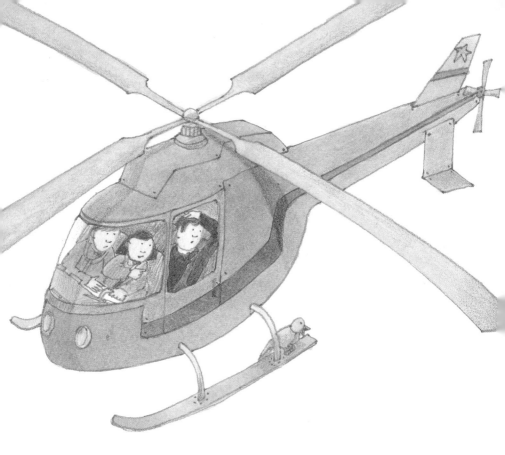

A much bigger helicopter than before.

'I've got it!' said Mr Mack. 'The best way out — is the way that he came in!'

Sam wished that they'd thought of that sooner — before they'd taken down his bedroom wall.

The helicopter circled lower and lower.

The hippo stirred uneasily. It stood up on the bed.

There was a CREAK . . .
   and a louder CREAK . . .
      and a very loud CREAK.
The bedroom floor began to collapse
very slowly.
The hippo glided gently down and
walked into the garden through the french
windows.

The garden emptied. Everyone ran away.
Even the helicopter had flown off.

The hippo gazed around the garden,
licked its large lips with an extra large
tongue — and began to eat the hankies one
by one. Mum was too astonished to stop it.
The hippo gobbled up every single hankie.

'Handkerchieves!' said Sam. 'So that's
what hippos like to eat!'

'I don't believe it!' said Dad.

The hippo gave a loud hiccup,
and walked over to the pond. *GULP . . .
GULP . . . GURGLE . . . GURGLE . . .*
It drank every drop of water in the pond.

'I've had enough of this,' said Sam,
unfastening the empty washing-line. He tied
it round the hippo's neck. 'Walkies,' he said
and led it out into the road.

Sam walked all the way to the zoo —
which was where they were trying to take
the hippo anyway. The hippo seemed very
happy to arrive. It settled down on a huge
straw bed.

'It's all right for you,' said Sam sadly.
'You've got somewhere to sleep.'

The zoo-keeper felt sorry for Sam.
'Perhaps you'd better stay with me tonight,'
he offered. So Sam slept in a spare bed at
the zoo until his bedroom was repaired.

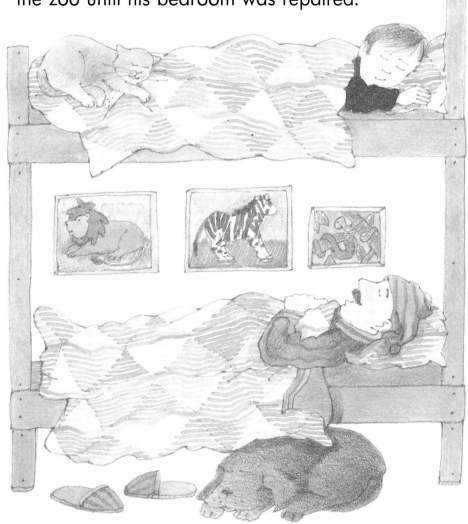

While he was there he learnt one important thing — that hippos *don't* eat hankies. At least not every day!

The zoo-keeper fixed a sign on Sam's bedroom door. It said: CHIEF HIPPO KEEPER.

'That's to remind you of what happened,' he told Sam. But Sam knew that he never would forget the day the hippo landed.